The SPORTS CLUB

Soccer

Jason Page

TWO CAN

PRINCETON ■ LONDON

Published in the United States and Canada by
Two-Can Publishing LLC
234 Nassau Street
Princeton, NJ 08542

www.two-canpublishing.com

© 2000, 1999 Two-Can Publishing

For information on Two-Can books and multimedia, call
1-609-921-6700, fax 1-609-921-3349, or visit our Web site at
http://www.two-canpublishing.com

Created by
act-two
346 Old Street
London EC1V 9RB

Text: Jason Page
Editor: Jacqueline McCann
Assistant editor: Lucy Arnold
Art director: Belinda Webster
Designers: Helen Holmes and Joanna Pocock
Consultant: Graham Ramsay, Maryland State Youth
  Soccer Association
Computer generated figures: Jonatronix
Computer illustrations: Mel Pickering
Picture research: Jenny West
Production: Adam Wilde

'Two-Can' is a trademark of Two-Can Publishing.
Two-Can Publishing is a division of Zenith Entertainment plc,
43-45 Dorset Street, London W1H 4AB.

HC ISBN 1-58728-0019
SC ISBN 1-58728-0035

HC 1 2 3 4 5 6 7 8 9 10 02 01 00
SC 1 2 3 4 5 6 7 8 9 10 02 01 00

Photographic credits: Action Images p12, p14, p18, p22, p26,
p29 (bottom left); Allsport p5, p10, p16, p24, p29 (bottom right);
Colorsport p20, p28 (bottom), p29 (top); Empics p19, p27, p28 (top);
PA News p21; Popperfoto p8

Covers: Allsport (top left & bottom); Colorsport (top right); Action Images (back)

Printed in Hong Kong by Wing King Tong

Contents

Words in **bold** in the text are explained here, along with other useful soccer terms.

Getting started

" Hi, I'm your coach and it's my job to help you master the basic skills you need to play **soccer** – the world's most popular team game! All you need is an open space, a ball, and some friends, and you're ready to start training. "

What you need

All the players in a team wear the same color jersey, called a uniform, to show they are on the same side. Often, players have a number printed on the back of their jersey. For outdoor games, you need shoes with cleats that grip the **field**, and a soccer ball!

Check your cleats before each game to make sure that they're not worn down.

Choose a soccer ball that is right for your size (under 9s use a size 3 and under 12s use a size 4).

Shin pads protect the fronts of your legs.

Long socks help to hold the shin pads in place.

Warming up

A good warm-up is essential before a game. Always loosen up and stretch your muscles to avoid a painful injury. First, jog around the field or skip for a few minutes, then try these simple thigh and ankle exercises. End with a short sprint and you'll be ready to start playing. To pick up tips, watch how other teams warm up before a game!

To stretch your thigh, hold your ankle and gently pull it toward your buttocks. Count to five, then relax. Now stretch your other leg.

To exercise your ankle, stretch one leg out in front of you. Roll your foot around in a circle while you count to ten. Do the same with your other foot.

Juggling fun

Now that you've warmed up, practice controlling the ball. See how long you can keep the ball in the air using only your feet, thighs, head, and chest. Why not ask a friend to time you? Try not to touch the ball with your arms or hands because this isn't allowed in soccer.

Practice short kick-ups. Lean back and bend your knees a little. Drop the ball onto your foot and kick it firmly with the top of your shoe ten times.

Now, bounce the ball with your thigh. When you can bounce the ball ten times in a row, try keeping the ball in the air using your head and chest.

Kicking the ball

Before a game, practice **passing** the ball back and forth with a friend. Start by kicking the ball with the inside of your foot. Then vary your technique by using other parts of your foot. This will help you to get a feel for the ball.

The safest way to kick the ball is with the inside of your foot, not with your toes. Aim for the middle of the ball to keep it low in the air.

inside of foot
instep
sole
outside of foot

By using different parts of your foot you can control the ball, or make it go in different directions. Use the inside, outside, instep, and sole of your foot.

◄ Good team spirit helps you to play well and enjoy yourself at the same time. Practice the skills and tactics in this book and you'll be able to play a great team game with your friends.

HOT TIPS
Don't be afraid of the ball – get used to it and have confidence in your own ability.

5

Meet the team

"In High School a team is made up of 11 players. The main positions are striker, midfielder, defender or goalkeeper. In Elementary School it is best to play 4 versus 4 or 7 versus 7. There are less rules and you get more chances to shoot and pass. Most children play 'street soccer' or small-sided soccer. "

Team formation

A coach may decide to make his team more attacking, by using more players as strikers. He may decide to play a more defensive game by using more defenders. The most common **formation** uses four defenders, four midfielders, and two strikers, so it's known as the 4-4-2 formation.

▶ It's the start of the match and the blue team is in its own half. The players are in a 4-4-2 formation. This line-up shows a good balance between attack and defense.

Strikers

It's our job to score goals against our opponents. Strikers need to be speedy and sneaky to outwit the other team's defense and get into a good position to shoot. We must be deadly accurate and able to shoot with both feet.

Attack
Two strikers stay forward. They rarely come back deep into their own half.

Ben
striker

Kim
midfielder

Raj
midfielder

Sue
defender

Jon
defender

Julie
goalkeeper

Left field
Players on the left-hand side of the field usually prefer to kick with their left feet.

Guarding the goal
The goalkeeper stays close to the goal. She must be alert and on guard at all times.

Midfielders

It's up to us to feed the ball to the strikers, or take a shot ourselves! If we lose possession of the ball, we race back to defend our own half, so we have to be really fit.

Defenders

Our job is to prevent the other team from reaching our penalty box and scoring. To do this we have to **tackle** and steal the ball, or kick it away to safety.

Raj

Matt

Kim

Dan

Jon

Tom

Sue

Sean

Goalkeeper

I'm the goalie, or keeper. When all else fails, it's up to me to stop the ball going into my goal. I have to be quick and brave. I am the only player on my team allowed to use my hands or arms to make saves, but I can only use them in my penalty box.

Julie

Liz
striker

Matt
midfielder

Dan
midfielder

Midfield
Four midfielders cover a large part of the field. They attack and defend.

Tom
defender

Sean
defender

Defense
Four strong defenders guard their half of the field and protect the goalkeeper.

Right field
Players on the right-hand side of the field usually prefer to kick with their right feet.

The rules

" I'm the **referee**, but call me Ref for short. If a player breaks the rules, he commits a **foul** and I blow my whistle to stop the game. I may award a **free kick**, or show a **yellow card** as a warning. A **red card** means you're off – I'm the one in charge on the **field**! "

▲ During the 1998 **World Cup**, the England **midfielder** David Beckham was shown the red card.

The field

The aim of the game is to score as many goals as possible. An adult game will last for 90 minutes whereas your game will go for 60 to 70 minutes. Midway through the game there's a break called **half-time**. All the action takes place on a **soccer** field. Let's take a look...

Goal line
If the ball crosses this line, the Ref will award a corner kick or a **goal kick**.

Goal
If the whole ball crosses the goal line inside the goal, you've scored!

Goal area
The goalie takes a goal kick from this box.

Center circle
At **kick-off**, your opponents may not enter this circle until you've kicked the ball.

Center spot
Kick off from here at the start of the game, after a goal, and after half-time.

Halfway line
Players must be in their own half of the field before kick-off.

Corner
Place the ball here to take a **corner kick**.

Touchline
When you kick the ball over this line, the Ref gives a **throw-in** to the other team.

Penalty area
The **goalkeeper** may handle the ball inside this box. If you commit a **foul** here, the Ref may award a **penalty kick** against you!

Penalty spot
Take a penalty from here.

Penalty arc
During a penalty, only a player taking a penalty is allowed in this area.

Fouls and free kicks

What is a foul?

1 A **tackle** where you touch your opponent before you touch the ball
2 pushing, kicking or holding onto your opponent
3 tackling from behind
4 touching the ball with your arms or hands
5 **obstruction** – getting in your opponent's way.

What happens next?

If you commit a foul accidentally, the Ref awards an **indirect free kick** to the other team. If the Ref thinks that the foul was deliberate, he gives a **direct free kick**.

Indirect free kick
The ball bounces higher than Sean was expecting and it's a **hand-ball**! The Ref awards an indirect free kick to the other team.

Direct free kick
As Raj sprints with the ball, a red **defender** deliberately tackles him from behind. The Ref gives a direct free kick to Raj's team.

The red team takes the indirect free kick. They must pass the ball at least once before they can take a shot. It's a goal!

Liz takes the direct free kick for her team. She **shoots** straight at the goal and scores! Well done, Liz!

Offside rule

When a teammate behind you **passes** the ball forward, there must be at least two opposition players level with, or between, you and the goal. Otherwise, you're **offside** and the Ref will give the other team a free kick.

This rule doesn't count if:

1 you are in your own half
2 you are behind the ball
3 you receive the ball from a throw-in, a corner kick or a goal kick.

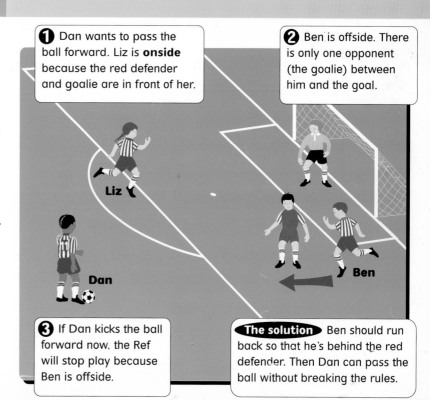

1 Dan wants to pass the ball forward. Liz is **onside** because the red defender and goalie are in front of her.

2 Ben is offside. There is only one opponent (the goalie) between him and the goal.

Liz

Dan

Ben

3 If Dan kicks the ball forward now, the Ref will stop play because Ben is offside.

The solution Ben should run back so that he's behind the red defender. Then Dan can pass the ball without breaking the rules.

Dribbling and turning

❝ Now it's time to improve your skills. Let's start with **dribbling**, that's **soccer** speak for dodging past **defenders** with the ball! Once you've mastered the basics, you'll be able to run rings around the opposition. **❞**

▲ Mia Hamm of the USA shows off her dribbling skills against China in the 1999 Women's **World Cup**.

Basic dribbling

The secret of good dribbling is not to kick the ball too hard — it should never be more than one step in front of you. Follow the ball, tapping it forward with the sides of your feet. Remember that if you can't reach the ball, you can't control it.

Kim uses both the inside and outside edges of her shoes to control the ball. She keeps her body over the ball and looks out for teammates who are free.

Kim needs more dribbling practice. She has kicked the ball too far ahead of her, making it easy for her opponent to steal it.

Stop turn

A great way to escape from an opposition player when you're dribbling is to change direction suddenly. Here's how it's done! Hop over the ball, then stop it using the heel or sole of your shoe. Quickly turn round, then race off in the same direction as the ball.

Dan has the ball, but an opponent is closing in on him. Suddenly, Dan stops running. He steps over the ball, then stops it dead with his foot.

Dan pushes the ball behind him, then turns and sprints off in a different direction. The red defender is left wondering what has happened!

Faking

Faking is pretending that you are about to turn one way, then turning another. To fool an opponent, try glancing in the wrong direction, dropping your shoulder or twisting your body. Here's Liz in action…

1 Liz is dribbling up the field toward a red defender who is **blocking** her path. Notice the way she keeps the ball close to her feet — good work, Liz!

2 As she gets closer to the red player, Liz drops her right shoulder to make it look as though she is turning to her right. The defender falls for the trick.

3 Quick as a flash, Liz turns to her left, using the outside of her left foot to control the ball. The red player moves to his left, but Liz dodges past him and sprints away.

Inside hook

When there's a defender hot on your tail, try this move. Use the inside of one foot to hook the ball, while you turn on the heel of the other foot.

Raj leans slightly to one side. He stretches for the ball and hooks it with the inside of his right foot.

Raj makes a half turn on his left foot and speeds off in the other direction with the ball.

HOT TIPS
Never dribble in your own penalty area – it's too risky! Show off your skills in the midfield, or near the goal you are attacking.

IN TRAINING!

To test your dribbling skills, set up a row of traffic cones (or you could use sweaters) approximately two yards apart. Then practice dribbling the ball in and out of the obstacles.

Vary your pace by speeding up and slowing down. When you reach the last obstacle in the line, turn around and dribble the ball back to the beginning again.

Passing

" **Passing** is vital for **midfielders** like me, but it's a skill that all players must learn. Passing the ball accurately between teammates is the key to scoring goals. So pay attention and I'll show you how it's done! "

▲ Juan Veron of Argentina is the 'brains' of his team. He sets up many attacks with his clever passing.

Short pass

If a teammate nearby is in a better position than you, pass the ball! A short pass along the ground is easy. All you need to do is practice controlling the ball. One other thing — only use this type of pass if there is a clear path between you and your teammate.

Raj places his non-kicking foot next to the ball and turns his body toward the target. Watch how he keeps his upper body and head over the ball.

Raj swings his leg and strikes the middle of the ball to keep the pass low. You can use the inside or outside of your foot for this shot.

Chip pass

A chip is a short pass that lifts the ball high into the air. Use this technique to pass to someone nearby when there's an opposition player in the way. With practice, you'll be able to pop the ball over your opponent's head so that it lands at your teammate's feet.

Matt's non-kicking foot is beside the ball. With his other foot, he stabs down beneath the ball and follows the ball through for extra power.

Matt chips the ball to Ben, over the head of the opposition player.

HOT TIPS

Lean forward for a short pass, but for a lofted pass, or a chip, lean backward to make the ball go further.

Lofted pass

A lofted pass is a long, high pass. It is used by **defenders** and midfielders to send the ball upfield. It's also a good pass to use when you take a **corner kick**. A lofted pass is more risky than a short pass because it's harder to control where the ball lands, especially on a windy day!

Jon places his non-kicking foot just behind and to the side of the ball. He strikes the bottom of the ball with his instep and follows through.

Dan

Jon

Jon clears the ball out of his own half and it reaches Dan in midfield. That's good defending, Jon!

Wall pass

The wall pass is also called the 'one-two'. It's a trick that two attacking players use to overcome a single defender. They pass the ball quickly between themselves.

❶ Ben runs with the ball straight toward the defender. At the last moment, he passes the ball to Liz.

❷ Ben keeps running past the defender into an open space. The defender follows the ball toward Liz.

❸ As soon as the ball reaches Liz, she taps it into the open space. Ben meets the ball and sprints toward the goal. Make sure you're **onside**, Ben!

IN TRAINING!

This drill helps to improve the timing and accuracy of your passing – you'll need a friend. Place five cones one yard apart on the ground.

Slowly dribble the ball around the outside of the cones. Pass the ball to your friend through a gap in the cones. Keep walking as your friend dribbles the ball and passes it back to you through another gap. Gradually speed up and try passing to each other while you jog.

Receiving the ball

❝ Now you've learned how to **pass** the ball, you need to know how to receive it. Let me show you how to use your feet, thighs, and chest to cushion the ball so that it doesn't bounce away from you. **❞**

▲ Edgar Davids, who plays for the Juventus team, is a skillful **midfielder**. Here he controls the ball on his chest.

Feet first

When the ball is rolling along the ground, you can stop it with your foot. This is the most straightforward way to receive the ball. Lift your foot slightly off the **field** and turn it sideways to meet the ball. As the ball hits your shoe, draw back your foot to absorb the impact.

You can use either side of your foot. Here, Dan uses the inside of his foot to meet the middle of the ball.

As the ball reaches Dan, he draws his foot back. This stops the ball from bouncing off his shoe.

In the air

If the ball is in the air, you can receive it with your thigh. Just as the ball lands, relax your leg muscles – this will take some of the power out of the ball's flight. The higher up your thigh the ball lands, the more easily you will be able to control it, so don't let it bounce off your knee!

Kim moves into position, keeping her eyes on the ball. She lifts up her arms to help her to balance.

As Kim makes contact with the ball, she brings her leg down gently. Easy does it, Kim – don't tense up!

Chest trap

Use your chest to control a high ball that's dropping down in front of you. Line yourself up to meet the ball and keep your hands out of the way — you don't want to give away a **hand-ball**! You can control the direction of the ball by twisting your body as the ball lands.

Kim faces the ball and pushes out her chest to meet it. She doesn't take her eyes off the ball for a second!

As the ball lands on Kim's chest, she lets her body sag back and go slack. The ball drops neatly to her feet!

What a catch!

You're not allowed to catch the ball with your hands, but you can try catching it with your feet! Use this skillful move to receive a ball in the air that's almost out of reach. You'll need to practice!

Dan stretches out his leg toward the ball, using his arms to balance. His toe points up and outward.

HOT TIPS
To stop a ball that's rolling gently along the ground, place the sole of your foot on top of the ball and wedge it down.

Dan catches the ball perfectly in the curve of his instep and gently guides the ball to the ground.

IN TRAINING!

Here's an easy drill for practicing ball control. Stand in front of a friend and ask him to throw or kick a ball to you. Ask him to vary the height and power of each pass without telling you what he is going to do.

Use your feet, thighs, and chest to cushion the ball as it comes toward you. Try to make the ball land at your feet each time. If the ball bounces back to the thrower three times, swap over!

Heading

66 It's time to start using your head! Hitting the ball with your head is called **heading** the ball. It shouldn't hurt a bit, but if it does, you're not doing it properly! Try practicing with a soft ball at first, to get used to it. 99

▲ Michelle Akers is good at heading the ball and was an important player in the USA **World Cup**-winning team.

Basic header

As the ball comes toward you, position yourself underneath it and keep your eyes open until the last second. Then strike the ball with the middle of your forehead. Thrust your head forward using your neck muscles. Keep your mouth closed or you may bite your tongue!

Tom pulls back his neck and upper body as he prepares to head the ball. He keeps his eyes open so that he can time his move perfectly.

Tom hits the ball between his eyebrows and hairline. He sends the ball forward by pushing with his neck muscles. That didn't hurt at all!

Defensive header

Defenders head the ball to keep it away from their goal. Often, two players go for the ball. Then, defenders jump to meet the ball first and thrust themselves forward to head the ball with extra force. The more powerful the header, the further up the **field** the ball will travel.

Sue times her run-up carefully. She wants to make contact with the ball when she is at the highest point in her jump.

Sue jumps at exactly the right time and she reaches the ball before a **striker** who's taller than her. Good timing is more important than being tall!

Attacking header

Accuracy is crucial when you're going for goal. You can control and change the direction of the ball by flicking or nodding your head just as you make contact. It can take a slight touch to send the ball into the goal. Again, timing is the key to success!

Ben moves into position to meet a powerful **corner kick**. This is a good chance to use his head to score!

As Ben touches the ball, he flicks his head toward the goal. Hopefully, the ball will go into the back of the net.

TOP TACTICS

Defenders need to head the ball high and far to clear it from the **goalbox**. It also pays to know where your teammates are.

❶ The red striker takes a shot at goal. Sean gets into position and is ready to clear the ball to safety.

❷ Sean sees that Raj is in a good position. Sean intercepts the ball and heads it to his teammate.

❸ Raj runs up the field with the ball to launch a counter-attack against the reds.

Sean

Raj

IN TRAINING!

Ask a friend to stand behind the goal and chip or throw the ball over the crossbar – that's the bar that runs along the top of the goal. Your job is to try to score using your head.

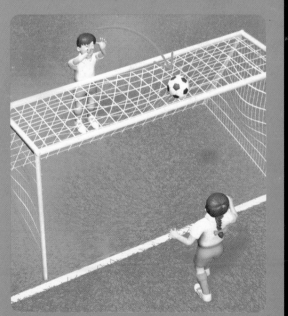

When you've scored five goals, swap positions with your friend. Once you've got the hang of it, you could ask another friend to play goalie – that should make things a lot more difficult!

Shooting

▲ Romario was a deadly **striker** who helped Brazil win the 1994 **World Cup**. Here he shoots against Sweden.

> **"** When you have a chance to score, take it! Stay calm and choose your target. Kick the ball hard and aim as far away from the **goalie** and the **defenders** as you can. Not every shot will go in, but the more you practice, the better you'll become! **"**

Low driven shot

When you're going for a goal, aim to send the ball just inside one of the posts. If you're feeling more daring, try to drive the ball straight past the keeper's legs. Keep the ball low — any goalie will tell you that powerful, low balls are the most difficult ones to save.

Liz's non-kicking foot is beside the ball. Liz swings her kicking foot back behind her. She aims to kick the middle of the ball with her instep.

Liz strikes the ball well. She swings her leg all the way through, after the ball. This follow-through makes her shot extra powerful.

Swerve shot

The aim of this shot is to make the ball spin when you kick it so that it swerves as it flies through the air. This type of shot is often used for taking **direct free kicks** and **penalty kicks**. Once you've got the knack, it's deadly!

Ben wants to curve the ball to the right, so he aims for the left-hand side of the ball. He strikes the ball with the outside of the top of his shoe.

As Ben's foot connects with the ball, the ball spins to the right. With a bit of luck, the ball will curve away from the keeper — straight into the goal!

Accuracy is everything when it comes to shooting, so you'll need to practice. Use chalk to draw six squares on a wall and number them 1 to 6. **Shoot** at the squares, starting at 1.

Try to hit each square in turn. Then practice shooting at the squares from different distances and angles.

The wall

▼ This is David Beckham in action for England, swerving the ball around a '**wall**' of Italian players in a qualifying round of the 1998 **World Cup**.

TOP TACTICS

A lot of work is needed to build an attacking move. This tactic shows how a team can work together to create a goal-scoring opportunity.

HOT TIPS
Be prepared for the ball to **deflect**, or bounce, off the keeper or the post. Go after the ball and follow up your shot!

❷ Kim passes to Liz, who is **onside** and in the clear.

Kim

Ben

Liz

❶ Ben starts the move by **passing** to Kim. Then Ben runs upfield.

Ben

❸ Liz crosses the ball back to Ben, who is in a prime position to shoot. Goal!

Defending

❝ When it comes to stopping the opposite team from scoring, everyone can help, not just the **defenders**! Everyone needs to be good at **tackling** and **marking** — two important defensive skills. Let me explain... ❞

▲ The defender, Jaap Stam, climbs highest to head the ball clear of danger for Holland against Argentina.

Marking

There are two different ways of marking. You can mark an opponent, which means that wherever that player goes, you go too. Or you can mark part of the **field**, defending that part against any opposition player who enters it.

Sue marks her opponent by staying as close to him as possible. She can touch him, but she must not push or hold him. That would be a **foul**!

This time Sue marks part of the field. Notice how Sue stays between the goal and the red attacker. She watches him closely and blocks his path wherever he moves.

Basic tackle

To tackle well, you need lots of practice and confidence. You may only tackle when your opponent has the ball, and remember — kick the ball, not your opponent! Use the inside of your shoe and try to push the ball behind your attacker.

Jon bends his knees and positions his body over the ball. He uses his bodyweight to help him push the ball over the red attacker's foot.

Jon has beaten his opponent and he sprints away. Now he needs to chase after the ball and control it!

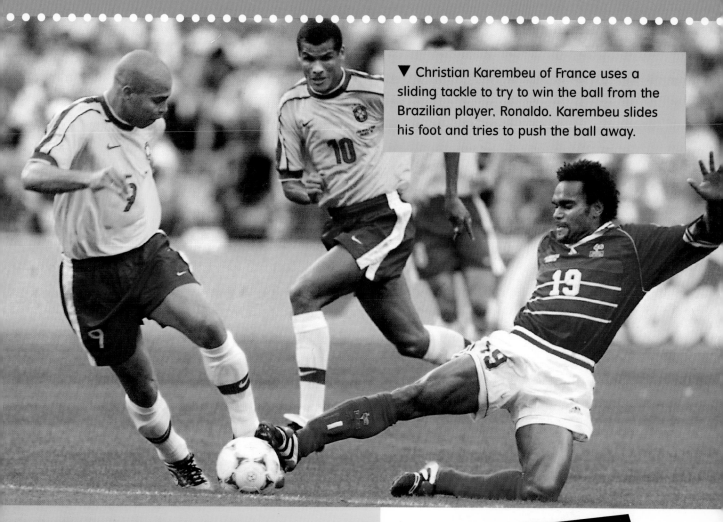

▼ Christian Karembeu of France uses a sliding tackle to try to win the ball from the Brazilian player, Ronaldo. Karembeu slides his foot and tries to push the ball away.

Blocking

When your opponent is about to **shoot**, try to **block** the path of the ball with your body. Be brave! Turn sideways and raise your leg to meet the ball. As soon as the ball bounces off you, be ready to race after it and regain possession.

Sue

Sue waits until the last moment to make her move. She wants to be sure that the red attacker will shoot.

Sue blocks the shot with her leg. Now she needs to watch where the ball goes and try to reach it first.

IN TRAINING!

Here's a drill that helps you to polish your tackling skills. All you need is a friend and two soccer balls. The idea is to protect your own ball while you tackle your opponent and try to steal his ball.

Every time you capture your opponent's ball, you win a point. Every time you lose your own ball, you lose a point. The first person to reach ten points is the winner!

Goalkeeping

Goalkeepers often notice things that other players miss, which is why you often see us shouting out instructions. But a goalie's main job is to protect the goal and stop the other team from scoring. Here's how it's done...

▲ Kasey Keller, the USA goalkeeper, dives to save a difficult low shot at the foot of his team's goalpost.

Catching high shots

You're the only player on the **field** who is allowed to touch the ball with her hands during play. Even then, you're only allowed to handle the ball inside your own goal area! Here's a tip — try to catch the ball in front of your face and don't stretch for the ball unless you have to.

Julie positions herself in line with the ball. Her hands are held high and her thumbs are almost touching. Watch the ball, Julie!

As Julie catches the ball, she pulls it down toward her tummy. She bends over the ball to protect it with her body. Hold on tight!

Catching low shots

Low shots are the hardest to save. The trick is to move your whole body behind the ball, not just your hands. If you have time, bend down on one knee. Lean forward so that you're ready to dive on top of the ball if it bounces away from you. Don't take your eyes off the ball!

An attacker sends a low ball Julie's way. Quick as a flash, she kneels down to stop the shot. Julie's palms face outward to meet the ball.

As the ball reaches Julie, her leg is side-on to the ball. She cups both hands and scoops the ball up to her chest. Another great save!

Clearing the ball

You won't always be able to catch the ball with your hands. When you can't catch it, clear it! Punch the ball as hard as you can toward one of your **defenders**. If you can't punch the ball, try to hit it out of play, either by sending it over the **crossbar** or by tapping it over the goal line.

This ball is too high to catch, so Julie jumps in the air, reaches the ball, and tips it over the top of the crossbar.

Julie dives to save the ball and just reaches it with her fingertips. She pushes it around the goalpost and across the goal line.

Narrowing the angle

A goalie faced with a single attacker should come out of the **goalbox** toward the ball. This makes it more difficult for the **striker** to score.

❶ Julie is standing too far back in goal. This shot isn't going to be easy to save – the red striker has a wide area to aim at!

❷ This time, Julie comes forward. She puts the striker under pressure because he has less space to aim at. Nice work, Julie!

IN TRAINING!

If you like playing in goal, try this exercise. Stand in the middle of the goal. Ask four friends, each holding a ball, to stand in a row about three yards in front of you. Ask each friend to throw his or her ball in turn, so that it bounces just in front of your goal line. Your job is to stop each ball crossing the line.

If you think you can handle this, try turning your back to your friends. Now ask them to shout out as they throw the ball. Quickly turn around and try to stop the ball.

Dead ball

66 When the **referee** blows the whistle, it means that the ball is 'dead' and play must stop immediately. There are lots of different ways to get the ball back in play. Here are several **dead-ball** skills you'll need to learn... **99**

▲ Fabien Barthez, the French keeper, swoops down on the ball to take a long **goal kick**.

Throw-in

If one team hits the ball over the touchline, the Ref awards a **throw-in** to the other team. Usually, the referee's assistant, called the linesman, decides where the ball crossed the line. The quicker you take a throw-in, the better — it keeps the opposition on their toes!

A red player hits the ball over the touchline, so the blue team wins a throw-in. The linesman shows Dan where he should take it.

Dan stands behind the line with both feet on the ground. Dan leans back for extra power. He must throw the ball over his head with both hands.

Corner kick

When a player hits the ball over his own goal line, the Ref gives a **corner kick** to the other team. This is a good chance to score! Often, the best kind of corner kick is a high ball that drops down into the goal area. Here, the attackers are at the ready to head the ball into goal.

Raj tries to pass the ball to Liz, but a red **defender** intercepts the ball and hits it over his own goal line. The Ref awards a corner.

Kim takes the corner. She lofts the ball high in the air and it drops down toward Ben. It's Ben's job to head the ball into the goal. Go for it, Ben!

DON'T FORGET
You must not kick a dead ball until the Ref has blown the whistle to signal that play may continue.

Goal kick

When a player hits the ball over his opponent's goal line, the Ref awards a goal kick to the opponent's team. The kick may be taken from anywhere inside the goal area and by any player. While the kick is being taken, no opposition players are allowed in the goal area.

goal line

A red **striker** takes a shot at goal, but the ball sails just over the **crossbar** and crosses the goal line. It's a goal kick to the blues!

Julie

Julie takes a short run-up and sends a long, high ball upfield. The players on the halfway line run toward the ball and jump up to try and win it.

Penalty kick

When a player commits a serious **foul** inside his own penalty area, the Ref blows the whistle — it's a **penalty kick** to the other team. One player kicks the ball from the penalty spot and tries to score. During this shot all other players must stay outside the penalty area and penalty arc.

Ben

Liz

Liz takes the penalty. She takes a short run-up and kicks a low ball toward the goal corner. As she kicks the ball, the other players run forward. The ball hits the post and rebounds toward Ben, who scores!

TOP TACTICS

The referee has awarded a **direct free kick** to the blue team, just outside the penalty area. This means that they can **shoot** straight at goal. The red players form a **wall** in front of the goal to **block** the shot, but the blue team has a plan…

❶ Both Dan and Kim run toward the ball from different directions.

Kim

Dan

❷ Dan reaches the ball first but jumps over it. Kim arrives a moment later and shoots.

❸ The reds think that Dan is going to take the kick. The goalie moves to intercept his kick, giving Kim's shot a clear route to the goal!

Advanced play

66 Once you've got to grips with the basic tactics, you can start learning more advanced **soccer** skills. These moves take a lot of practice, as you are about to discover! Perfecting them is what makes a soccer player a soccer hero. **99**

▲ Manchester United's Henning Berg throws himself forward to meet the ball with a dynamic diving header.

Volley shot

Kicking the ball while it's in the air is called volleying. If you're a **striker**, it's a useful skill to master. Don't wait for the ball to bounce — kick it in midair, just before it lands. The **goalie** and the **defenders** will have less time to prepare.

Ben keeps his body and kicking knee over the ball to stop it rising. Ben's toes are pointed down to keep the ball low.

Side volley

To perform this tricky variation on the volley, stand sideways to the ball. As the ball approaches, pivot on one leg and swing up your kicking foot. Keep your eye on the ball, lean back and use your arms to help you to balance.

Ben keeps his head forward, even though he is leaning back. This helps to keep his shot low.

Diving header

For this header, you launch yourself at the ball to give your header extra power. Timing is everything. Get it wrong and you may dive nose-first into the **field**!

The ball comes toward Raj below head height. Raj pushes with his left leg and hurls himself at the ball.

Raj does a brilliant diving header. He flicks his head sideways toward the goal and spreads out his arms to break his fall.

◀ Strength, timing, and good balance are needed to perform this overhead clearance. Here, Joe-Max Moore of the USA lifts his right foot high into the air while balancing with his left foot. He throws his body back and kicks the ball over his head behind him.

TOP TACTICS

Use the size of the field to your advantage. Here, the blue team creates space to attack by **passing** the ball out wide, to the edge of the field.

HOT TIPS

Remember your ABC – Accuracy, Balance, and Control! And never use a difficult shot if a simple one will do.

3 Kim sprints out wide, away from the other players. Raj passes to her so that she can dribble the ball all the way up the touchline.

Ben

Kim

Liz

2 Ben and Liz are running forward, but they are being **marked** closely by red defenders.

Raj

1 Raj **dribbles** the ball forward. He wants to pass to a teammate.

Hall of Fame

PELE

66 Every once in a while, an amazing soccer player comes along. He may be a goal-scorer, he may bring his country to **World Cup** victory, but one thing is sure, he must have talent. This is my list of the top five most talented players of all time. See if you agree. 99

Name Edson Arantes do Nascimento — but known to soccer fans everywhere as Pele!
Date of birth 21 October 1940
Country Brazil

Did you know? Pele is the youngest player ever to have received a World Cup winner's medal. He scored two goals in the 1958 final, when Brazil defeated Sweden 5-2.
Achievements Pele is the greatest player the world has ever seen. He helped Brazil win the World Cup three times. During his career, Pele played in 1,363 professional matches, scoring a record 1,281 goals!

HOT SHOTS
Brazil hold the World Cup record. They have won the trophy an incredible four times! The last time was in 1994.

BECKENBAUER

Name Franz Beckenbauer
Date of birth 11 September 1945
Country Germany

Did you know? Beckenbauer worked as an insurance salesman before he played professional soccer.
Achievements Beckenbauer played for West Germany's World Cup team in 1966 and 1970, and was team captain when they won in 1974. After making 103 appearances for his country, Beckenbauer retired. In 1984 he returned to the West German team as manager. Six years later, in 1990, he guided his players to another World Cup victory!

MARADONA

Name Diego Maradona
Date of birth 3 October 1960
Country Argentina

Did you know? Maradona's second goal against England in Mexico in 1986 was voted the greatest World Cup goal ever. He started the move in his own half, then dribbled past half of the English team, before scoring.
Achievements Maradona was only 16 when he first played for Argentina. He captained the team to the finals of the 1986 and 1990 World Cup tournaments. In 1986, Argentina won and Maradona was voted Player of the Tournament.

EUSEBIO

Name Eusebio Da Silva Ferreira – but known simply as Eusebio!
Date of birth 25 January 1942
Country Portugal

Did you know? A statue of Eusebio stands in his honour outside his old club, Benfica, in Lisbon, Portugal.
Achievements Eusebio helped Benfica win the Portuguese League seven times and the Portuguese Cup five times. He played for Portugal 46 times and scored 38 goals, nine of them during the 1966 World Cup.

GEORGE BEST

Name George Best
Date of birth 22 May 1946
Country Northern Ireland

Did you know? Before Best signed with Manchester United, several teams rejected him. They thought he was too skinny and weak!
Achievements Pele said that Best was the most talented player he had ever seen. Best helped Man Utd win the European Cup in 1968, when he was named European Soccer Player of the Year. In an FA Cup game in 1970, Best scored six goals! This record still stands today.

Soccer phrases

blocking Using your body or leg to stop the ball when your opponent takes a shot at goal.

corner kick When a defender kicks or deflects the ball over his own goal line, an attacker restarts the game by kicking the ball from the corner closest to where the ball crossed the goal line.

crossbar The horizontal bar that lies across the top of the goalposts.

dead ball A ball that has gone out of play.

defender A playing position, or a player who is part of the defensive team.

deflection A ball that has bounced off the goalpost, crossbar or another player.

direct free kick A free kick in which the player taking the kick may aim directly for the goal and score.

dribbling Running with the ball using the insides and outsides of your feet to tap it forward and keep it under control.

field A World Cup or full-size soccer field is usually 110 yards long by 70 yards wide. The touchlines must always be longer than the goal lines. Junior soccer players need to play on smaller fields with smaller goals — the field has to fit the players.

FIFA This stands for the Fédération Internationale de Soccer Association, which was created in Switzerland in 1904. FIFA is responsible for deciding the rules of the game of soccer and for organizing many international competitions, such as the World Cup.

formation Before a game, the coach decides where to place each member of the team on the field, as attackers or defenders. This line-up of players is known as the formation. The coach can make the formation of the team more attacking or more defensive.

foul To break one of the rules of soccer. A foul is sometimes called a violation.

free kick When the Ref gives a player a chance to kick the ball without interference from the other team.

goalkeeper A playing position, or the player who guards her team's goal. This player is also called the goalie, or keeper, and is the only player who can touch the ball with her hands when the ball is in play.

goal kick A kick taken by the goalie or a defender in their own goal area. It restarts the game after an attacking team has sent the ball over a defensive team's goal line.

goalbox The area in front of the goal.

half-time A short break in the middle of the match, so that players can rest and discuss tactics. When play resumes, the two teams swap ends of the field.

hand-ball It is a foul to touch the ball with your hands deliberately. If this happens, the Ref awards a free kick against your team.

heading Using your head to hit the ball.

indirect free kick A free kick in which the player taking the kick may not aim directly at goal. The ball must touch another player before a goal can be scored.

kick-off Each half of the game begins with a player kicking the ball from the center spot. The ball is also kicked from here after a goal has been scored.

marking Guarding an opponent to prevent her from getting the ball, or guarding an area of the field.

midfielder A playing position, or a player who runs upfield to attack, or downfield to defend, depending on how he is needed. Midfielders are also called halfbacks.

obstruction Deliberately getting in the way of an opponent and stopping him getting the ball without trying to play the ball yourself. This is a foul!

offside When a teammate behind you passes the ball forward, there must be at least two opponents level with, or between, you and the goal. If not, you're offside.

onside Having at least two opponents level with, or between you and the goal, when the ball is played forward.

passing Sending the ball to a teammate without using the hands or arms.

penalty kick When a defending team commits a foul in its own penalty area, the Ref allows an attacking player to kick the ball from the penalty spot.

red card A red card is given to a player who repeatedly commits a bad foul, and he is sent off the field.

referee The referee, or Ref, is in charge of the game. He makes sure that both teams play by the rules. The Ref also stops and starts the game.

shoot To try to score by kicking the ball at the opponent's goal.

soccer The word soccer is short for 'association soccer' which is the official name of the game.

small-sided games Games such as 4 against 4 and 7 against 7 are the best soccer games for young players. With fewer rules and fewer players, there are more chances to touch the ball.

striker A playing position, or a player who spends most time in the attacking half of the field, trying to score a goal.

tackling Using your feet to take the ball away from an opponent.

throw-in When a player kicks the ball over the touchline, a player from the other team throws the ball back into play. He must hold it in both hands and throw it over his head, keeping both feet on the ground.

wall A defensive barrier formed when several members of a team stand next to each other in order to block a free kick.

World Cup An international competition first held in 1930. It has been held every four years since — except in World War II.

yellow card The Ref shows a player the yellow card as a formal warning for bad behavior or for committing a foul.

Index

Help!

So you want to know more about playing soccer locally? Here are a few tips...

● Check local soccer stores, public libraries, and Yellow Pages to find organizations in your area.

● Call your State Youth Association. They can give you a list of local teams and organizations.

● Call your local YMCA or Recreation Department for soccer sign-up. This happens around late summer and early spring.

● Play in pick-up games at your local park. You'll make friends and learn about the sport.

● Finally, play for fun and play to learn.

Good luck and good soccer !

Useful addresses

USYSA (United States Youth Soccer Association)
899 Presidential Drive, Suite 117, Richardson, Texas 75081
Tel: 1-800-4-SOCCER

Canadian Soccer Association
Place Soccer Canada, 237 Metcalfe Street, Ottawa, Ontario K2P 1RS, Canada
Tel: 1-613-237-7678

Visit these Web sites:
www.soccer-sites.com
www.soccerclinics.com
www.reddingcal.com/ISKA/ISKA.htm